Balboa Press books may be ordered through booksellers or by contacting:

Balboa Press
A Division of Hay House
1663 Liberty Drive
Bloomington, IN 47403
www.balboapress.com
844-682-1282

ISBN: 979-8-7652-4081-6 (sc)
ISBN: 979-8-7652-4486-9 (hc)
ISBN: 979-8-7652-4082-3 (e)

Print information available on the last page.

Balboa Press rev. date: 08/31/2023

BALBOA.PRESS
A DIVISION OF HAY HOUSE

"Good afternoon!" said Coach May excitedly. "Instead of our regular PE, today we're going to learn about our power centers."

"Our what centers?" said Lee with a funny look.

"Power centers?" asked Ryan. "What is a power center?"

"Every person has seven main power centers along their spine," explained Coach May. "Discovering and practicing how to use these can help us when life gets challenging. The more we understand how to use our power centers, the stronger they become. Are you interested in learning more?"

"I am!" said Sonia.

"I guess," said Lee, crossing his arms. "But it sounds weird."

"Well, let's get weird, then," said Coach with a smile. "Lie down on the grass with me."

"Do you feel that?" Coach asked.

"Feel what?" a chorus of kids answered.

"The earth," Coach May replied.

The kids giggled.

Coach smiled and said, "If you close your eyes and slow down your breathing, you can feel that the earth is alive and that we are connected to its energy. This brings me to the first power center. It is located at the bottom of your spine. This is the center that connects you to everything and everyone."

"Everything? Everyone?" asked Carlos.

"Yep. Everything and everyone," Coach answered. "Whenever you are scared, this is where you should focus your attention. This center is a ruby-red color and can help you connect and feel safe. To practice, place your hands over the bottom of your spine and imagine a red circle. Now take a few deep breaths and say, 'I am safe. I am connected. I am supported.' The more you do this, the more you will feel a deep connection to the earth and everything on it."

"It feels good," said McKenna.

"I don't feel anything," said Ryan.

"That's OK. The more you practice, the stronger these centers will become," said Coach May enthusiastically. "The next center is right above the first one. It is a vibrant orange color. This is where creativity is stored. When you are feeling stuck, lost, or even lonely, this center helps you feel special and unique. We are individually wonderful. If you pay enough attention to this center, you will realize how fun it is to be you. Place your hand on this orange center and say, 'I am creative. I am unique. I feel happy.'"

"I feel tingly," said Sonia.

"The next center is really exciting," Coach said. "It is on your stomach, just below your chest. It is a sparkling yellow circle. It's like you have a miniature sun inside that you can connect to when you need strength and courage. The more you pay attention to this power center, the stronger you can feel," said Coach.

"Like a superhero who can punch through buildings?" said Joe super excitedly.

"Well, more of a warrior strength," said Coach May with a smile. "This is important because sometimes things happen that are out of our control, and we may need courage and strength to get through them."

"Like when someone is mean to you and you feel strong enough to ignore them and walk away?" asked Mckenna.

"Yes, that is a great example," said Coach. "We can't control what other people say or do, but we can control how we react. Spending time with this power center will help you become more resilient and able to react with a warrior's attitude. Place your hands on this yellow center and say, 'I am strong. I have control over my thoughts and behavior. I am confident.'"

"The next power center is farther up your spine, over your chest and heart," said Coach calmly. "This center is very important. It is a beautiful green color, and it is where your love comes from. Place your hands over your chest, imagine a green color, and then say, 'I want more love in my life—lots of love and happiness.' Doesn't that feel nice?"

"It does," said most of the girls with huge smiles.

"It's kinda girly," said Damion.

"Girly? Since when is love a girly thing?" asked Coach. "Love is for everyone. Open your heart, connect to this green center, and know you deserve love no matter who you are. Place your attention on your heart and say, 'I am worthy of love. I am capable of love. I give and receive love freely.'"

"Moving on, the next power center is on your throat, and it is light blue," said Coach May. "This power center helps you say what you are feeling. It can also help you speak kindly to others and know that your opinion matters. Place your hands gently over your throat and connect to this center when you feel like your voice doesn't matter—because it *does* matter."

"Even when my mom tells me to be quiet?" Ryan asked.

Coach looked over at Ryan and said, "No. This is not permission to talk back or speak after you've been asked to remain quiet. But if you feel as though nobody cares about what you have to say, put your attention here and say, 'What I feel matters. What I say matters. My voice and opinions are valuable.'"

"The next center is cool," said Coach. "It is located on your forehead. It is a magical dark-blue color, and this it is where your intuition is."

"What is intuition?" asked Joe.

"It is your inner knowing," Coach answered. "Have you ever been around someone who seems sad? They may not show it, but you sense that they are sad. Feeling intuition is different from observing with your ears and eyes. It is listening with an inner sense of knowing," explained Coach May.

Most of the kids seemed confused, so Coach May smiled and explained further. "Some superheroes have great intuition and can detect danger or know when someone needs help. We have that ability too, and the more we listen and tune in to it, the stronger it becomes. So if you have a bad feeling about someone, pay attention to this power center and listen to your body. If your body feels tight and wants to get away from this person, it might be your intuition letting you know that something is off so that you can stay alert. Does this make sense?"

"Yes," the kids agreed.

"Intuition is something all of us have access to. It just takes practice; you have to learn to trust your feelings," said Coach May. "Focus on your forehead and picture a dark-blue color. Now say, 'I trust my intuition. I pay attention to my feelings. I pay attention to how others are feeling. I trust and believe in myself.'"

"The final power center is at the top of your head and is a light-purple color. This center circles back to your first center. This power center connects you beyond just the earth. This is your connection to the universe through the stars, planets, and galaxies. You can focus on this center and imagine yourself in space, feeling bigger than life on Earth," explained Coach.

"I love space," said Carlos.

"I do too," said Anne.

"When you want to connect to the energy of everything, you can focus your attention on the top of your head and even the space above your head," Coach continued with enthusiasm.

"Place your attention on the space just above your head and say, 'I am connected to love. I belong here, and I am always supported. I feel light and peaceful when I am in this space,'" continued Coach May.

"These are the seven power centers. They are always available to help guide and support us on our journey," explained Coach May.

"It's like we have superpowers!" shouted Lee excitedly.

I belong here and I am always supported with love.
I trust my feelings.
What I say and feel matters.
I am filled with love.
I am confident with warrior strength.
I feel unique.
I am safe

And the kids all cheered. "We're super kids! We can do anything!"

A GUIDED MEDITATION

Gently close your eyes and take a few slow breaths. You are safe and loved.

Imagine a bright red light at the base of your spine. This is your root center. Say to yourself, "I am strong and grounded like a mighty tree. I am safe and protected."

Breathe in slowly, and breathe out slowly.

Move your attention to your lower belly, where there's a vibrant orange light. This is your sacral center. Say to yourself, "I am creative, unique, and fun. I love to explore and learn new things."

Breathe in slowly, and breathe out slowly.

Now, visualize a bright yellow light in your stomach. This is your solar plexus center. Say to yourself, "I am confident and brave. I believe in myself and my abilities."

Breathe in slowly, and breathe out slowly.

Imagine a gentle green light in your heart. This is your heart center. Say to yourself, "My heart is open and filled with love. I am worthy of love and happiness."

Breathe in slowly, and breathe out slowly.

Move up to your throat and picture a calm blue light. This is your throat center. Say to yourself, "I speak with courage and kindness. My words are powerful."

Breathe in slowly, and breathe out slowly.

Shift your focus to your forehead. Imagine a dark blue light there. This is your intuition center. Say to yourself, "I trust my feelings and listen to my inner knowing. I see and understand things clearly."

Breathe in slowly, and breathe out slowly.

Finally, move to the top of your head. Picture a radiant purple light. This is your crown center. Say to yourself, "I am connected to this incredible universe. I am a shining light of wisdom and love."

Breathe in slowly, and breathe out slowly.

Take a few more empowering breaths, and when you're ready, open your eyes. You are amazing!

Printed in the United States
by Baker & Taylor Publisher Services